Quentin Blake

PATRICK

COLLINS
PICTURE LIONS

First p   Britain
by Jonath   Cape Ltd in 1968
First published in Picture Lions in 1991
This edition published in 1993

9 8 7 6 5 4 3

Picture Lions is an imprint of the
Children's Division, part of HarperCollins
Publishers Limited, 77-85 Fulham Palace Road,
Hammersmith, London W6 8JB

Printed and bound in Singapore.

This is a story about a young man called Patrick, who set out from his house one day to buy a violin.

In the town the streets were full of stalls. One sold
vegetables, one sold fish and another sold clothes.

These stalls were very interesting but Patrick did not stop until he came to the one kept by Mr Onions. On his stall he had a broken jug, an old lamp, a mouse-trap and all sorts of things that people did not want any more.

"Have you a violin to sell?" asked Patrick.

"You're in luck," said Mr Onions, "I have just one."

Patrick bought the violin with his only silver piece.

He was so pleased that he ran as fast as
he could out into the fields.

When he got there he blew the dust off his violin.

Then he sat down by a pond and began to play a tune. As he played, the most extraordinary thing happened. One by one the fish in the pond began to jump out and fly about in the air. And what is more, they were all different colours and they were singing to the music.

Just then a girl and a boy came along the road.
Their names were Kath and Mick.

"Did you do that?" asked Mick, pointing to the fish
in the air. And Patrick said, "Yes."

Then he played another tune, and the string tying
Kath's hair turned into red ribbons and the laces in
Mick's boots turned into blue ribbons.

And so the three went down the road together.
Soon they came to an orchard of apple trees. Patrick
played his violin and the leaves on the trees changed
to all kinds of bright colours.

Instead of apples the trees began to grow pears and bananas and cakes and ice-creams and slices of hot buttered toast. Kath and Mick ran about among the trees and helped themselves to whatever they liked.

As they were eating, a flock of pigeons flew down
and Patrick played his violin again. The birds began
to sprout bright new feathers until they were the most
beautiful birds you have ever seen. Kath and Mick
fed them on crumbs of chocolate cake.

And they all got back to the town before dark.